# VISION
# COLLISION

**THINK • WRITE • BELIEVE • ACHIEVE**

## REAGAN B. NEVELS

Books may be ordered through booksellers or by contacting:
Leadership DevelopME, LLC
P.O. Box 481048
Charlotte, NC 28269
www.leadershipdevelopme.com
(704) 659-3882

ISBN 978-1-387-58274-7
www.lulu.com

Printed in the United States of America.

# Table of Contents

# Dedication

This book is dedicated to my family and friends. I hope to make you proud and serve as a shining example that you can do anything you dream of by putting God first and believing in yourself. I also wrote this book for young people, like myself.

With so many negative influences, this book is intended to have a positive influence on my generation. The purpose of writing this book is to share my hidden gifts and talents with the world. For many years, I've hidden it, but now, at the age of 12, I am convinced that I must share what I have with others.

This book is also dedicated to my Grandma, Frances Nevels, who passed away in the year of 2015. She taught me the value of wisdom, meekness, and remaining humble. I never heard her say an evil word and always served as a good example. She kept a smile on her face and possessed a good attitude. Grandma

Nevels was a great woman, and with immense strength, she completed everything with excellence.

# Acknowledgements

First, I want to thank God for the blessing, gifts, and talents. The idea of this book was inspired by God and completed with the strength provided in me.

Second, I want to thank my family and friends for the support on my journey to become a published author. My dad, Emmitt Nevels Jr.; my mom, Kacie Nevels; sisters, Paige and Grace, and my brother, Emmitt Nevels III. You all mean everything to me.

Lastly, I want to say thank you to Dr. Lawanne' S. Grant for encouraging me to write this book. She pushed me to pen what I wanted others to know, rather than writing what people wanted me to put down.

I must acknowledge that writing and publishing this book wasn't an easy journey. It required much sacrifice, but at the end, it was worth it all!

# Foreword

From the days of infancy, Reagan Benet Nevels has always been insightful with great wisdom to handle the stages of life. As you read this book, I am confident you will agree that she possesses wisdom far beyond the average twelve-year-old. She writes for a young audience, but many of the principles shared in this book can be applied to the adult life.

Reagan is a shining example that you can do anything you put your mind to. She stayed up long nights, spent hours in the library, and chose not to engage in leisure activities so that you would know what a vision collision is. She masterfully defines vision and explains what happens during the collision.

Reagan inspires you to identify what God sees for your life and to go after it with all you have. It's no doubt that this is another accomplishment causing Reagan's parents, siblings, immediate and extended family to be very proud of the young girl she is and the lady she will become. She is indeed a leader and visionary for her generation.

*Lawanne' S. Grant, Ph.D.*

# Introduction

Welcome to the world of Vision Collision. My name is Reagan Nevels, and I'll be your tour guide through the next few chapters. I'm 12 years old but nestled in this book is mature advice for people of all ages, both male and female. People tell me that they are amazed at the wisdom I have as a young girl. I'm always thinking of how to make everything in our lives collide together to have a positive impact.

I think it's important to know more about me as we get to know each other during your Vision Collision journey. I have thirteen cousins, seven aunts, six uncles, and much more extended "family." I consider extended family to be my mom's friends that we call auntie or dad's friends that we call uncle. I absolutely love school but also love to socialize. The social side of me sometimes gets me in trouble, causing my mom to give me "that side-eye look."

Family is very important to me, and I look for reasons to celebrate them. I creatively express my love during celebratory events such as birthdays, reunions, weddings, and recitals. Although I'm legally considered a child, I take great interest in the welfare of children. I enjoy helping them with dancing, completing homework, and involvement in extra-circular activities. My mom runs a daycare, and that's probably where I gained my love for children.

Unlike the average 12-year-old, I've been thinking a lot about life and how I want to start it. Of course, life has already begun but what I'm referring to is that, once life begins, I will be independent of my mom and dad. I dream about going to college, meeting influential people, and landing a career job that pays me lots of money. I want to try new things, but the problem is, how in the world do I put together all the ideas in my head?

My mom says that I am a very multifaceted individual. I think what she means is that I have many *visions* and I can do a whole lot of things well all at the same time. It's a wonderful thing to be multifaceted, but at some point in your life, you must choose where to channel your energy. The wisest direction to aim in is toward goals that will compliment who you want to be and what you want to do in the future.

As we walk hand in hand through the Vision Collision journey, expect to discover thoughts and ideas behind closed doors of your life. You'll have to be bold enough to knock on the door. In fact, some doors have to be forced or knocked down. Once it's opened, don't be afraid of all the potential you see in yourself. This is called *vision*.

After you see it, you have to go after it. Don't worry; remember, I'm only twelve years old. If I can focus on the vision of my life in the future, so can you. It doesn't matter how old or young you are. Regardless of your past accomplishments, there's always room for another vision to be fulfilled. Are you ready? Let's take the journey of fulfilling the vision for our lives together.

# Chapter 1
# What is VISION?

Vision, as a noun defined by Merriam-Webster Dictionary is, "the ability to see: site or eyesight; something that you imagine: a picture that you see in your mind; something that you see or dream especially as part of a religious or supernatural experience." It's amazing how several people can hear something and imagine different things. For example, you can hear that meat will be offered at dinner tonight; but there are so many types of meat. There is chicken, steak, lamb, beef and more. My vision of dinner may be fried chicken, while your vision of dinner might be a hamburger. You see, a vision is a mental image of what you perceive. It's your hopeful thoughts of something that can come to life. Having a vision gives you the awesome ability to create beautiful things and people. You can dream of the perfect picture. If you don't have a vision, you're in a dangerous space. As P.K. Bernard said, "A man without a vision is a man without a future. A man without a future will always return to his past."

I want to introduce you to my mom's sister, my Aunt Natalie. When she was seventeen years old, she had the vision to serve in the military. Even though she had a vision to go away, this was a very hard decision because she would be leaving her family and giving up some of the fun things she could do as a teenager. She had lots of decisions to make in order to fulfill her vision.

Ultimately, she decided to leave everything behind not knowing what was on the other side of her vision decision. She was getting ready to experience another side of life. Thinking she was just in high school, enjoying being a teenager and now she was on her way to become an active member of the military. I don't know if I've ever told you, but thank you, Auntie Natalie, for serving our country.

Here's a lesson I learned from Aunt Natalie's vision, you can't just show up, but you have to prepare to make your vision happen. She didn't know what this experience would be like when she got off the plane. To her surprise, she met with people screaming at her and telling her what to do. This was far from any interaction she had with other students or teachers at school. Following her vision was going to be tougher than she thought, but she kept at it because she imagined herself being successful in the military.

The funny thing is that she really didn't know what being successful in the military looked like. Yep! Our visions can be a little blurry at times, but we have to keep at it until our vision becomes clear, like Aunt Natalie's did. She could've quit, but she was brave. She stayed in the military until she fulfilled her vision. Aunt Natalie served 21 years for our country and retired at the age of 38 years old. She climbed the ladder in military ranks, earned a bachelor's degree, and achieved the success she imagined in her vision way back in high school.

George Bernard Shaw said in an Irish script, "Life isn't about finding yourself. Life is about creating yourself". I agree completely with George because I feel that in life you should always be evolving (getting better). Really, I love what George wrote because there is so much truth in every word, every letter, and every syllable. Creating yourself means that you have to make sure you color outside of the lines and step outside of your normal boundaries. Now, this doesn't mean that you will always get it right, but at least it will be easy to know exactly what to fix in order to create a better you.

I don't know about you, but I don't ever want to feel like I have a vision and don't strive to do it. Remember, a vision is that thing you dream or daydream about. It's the thinking that makes you so happy about how you'd feel if it actually happened or you can't stop thinking about your plans to make it happen. It really feels cool when you dream about something, and it actually happens. Has this ever happened to you? It has happened to me. It's called déjà-vu!

Now, there are some things that just happen, but other events in life require you to plan. In this case, we are going to plan ahead. By planning ahead, I mean writing down what you want to happen in the future. This is a good strategy because it allows you to see everything that you need to do and set time frames to get it. Let's be clear that I am only here to help you discover the vision that God has given and trusted you to make happen. Everyone is given some kind of vision by God, and He knows that you can accomplish it. Don't worry; there's a section at the end of this chapter for you to jot down your ideas. Follow the steps closely and take advantage of the opportunity to be inspired toward your vision.

You will be asked to identify three things you want to do and three things you want to become. From this list, you will pick one of each to discover your perfect combination. A perfect combination are two things that you can work on at the same time in order to get different yet successful results. For example, you might want to play a piano and as well become a scientist. Sounds good to me! While these are two different visions, the work you have to do can complement each other. You will have to attend school and get passing grades. Receiving passing grades may be your pass to make your parents allow you to attend late rehearsals or recitals to become an awesome pianist. You see how the visions collide. If you earn good grades, you earn participation in extra-curricular activities. There you have it! Two of your visions will come to past to make a perfect combination.

Do me a favor; throw yourself into this book. By this, I mean position yourself to receive the help. We'll do this together because after all, I've never written a book in my life. There's a lesson I'm learning as I put every letter and word on paper. In a very fun way, we'll decide what we should and should not do in order to accomplish purpose and see our vision become reality.

Later in the book, we are going to make a vision board that lays out our thoughts and processes to accomplishing what we see. It's always good to make a visual display of your goals.

As you journey through Vision Collision, remember that I wrote this book for you. I want you to be true to yourself. Don't write down what other people dream for you but who you dream of becoming. This can happen by answering questions like, what is *your* vision? What are the things you want to be successful at? What are your goals? What is your purpose? Guess what? You just envisioned yourself in the future and made the definition of vision more real to you.

Your thoughts, your dreams, and ambitions for the future are your visions. Although things might change in the future, but you should at least have a plan or idea of what your future holds. At the age of twelve,

I know that I will experience different stages in life and my visions may change. However, I believe that once you accomplish certain things, God will give you another vision. Every person should have some kind of dream or path to follow every day that you awake and go about your day. You should have goals and aspirations to have a clear direction as to what star you are reaching for.

I have many goals and visions for myself. I feel that I must accomplish them because they were brought to my mind for some reason and purpose. For example, I wanted to dance, and now I'm in my eighth year. Oh, by the way, many people think that dance isn't as sporty as football or basketball, but it takes strength, commitment, hard work, and perseverance just like all other sports. I wanted to play the piano about five years ago, and now not only do I play fluently, but I am also learning how to play the organ. I wanted to play tennis, and I played for about 2 years and mastered it at the age of 10. I wanted to do photography because I love to capture amazing moments. Now, I am able to tell a story through a photo and catch babies falling asleep with their dads like I always fell asleep in my dad's arms.

I'm able to show other young people the power of a picture and share the message to be careful of the pictures that you take and share with others because it tells a story about who you are. This is real because a lot of us are pressured to be on social media. Of course, the pressure is real, but we have to remember as young people that we are who we are, not because of how others look at us, but because of what we contribute to the world around us. Almost all kids my age have been on social media for several years now. I am actually not on any social media, which is hard to believe to my friends, but I would say that I am extremely social!

Lastly, I wanted to sew, and I started a business making scarves. You see, I've climbed a lot of mountains with a lot of mountains ahead. Every journey that has been and will be accomplished, started with a vision.

Once again, I always rely on God to help me see the vision He has for me. Check out 20 Christian quotes that Pamela Rose Williams provides. They really inspire me when it comes to vision:

> When I think of vision, I have in mind the ability to see above and beyond the majority. ~ Chuck Swindoll.

> Our vision is so limited we can hardly imagine a love that does not show itself in protection from suffering. The love of God did not protect His own Son... He will not necessarily protect us – not from anything it takes to make us like His Son. A lot of hammering and chiseling and purifying by fire will have to go into the process. ~ Elizabeth Elliott

➤ Moreover the word of the LORD came unto me, saying, Jeremiah, what seest thou? And I said, I see a rod of an almond tree. ~ Jeremiah 1:11 KJV

➤ We need a baptism of clear seeing. We desperately need seers who can see through the mist–Christian leaders with prophetic vision. Unless they come soon, it will be too late for this generation. And if they do come, we will no doubt crucify a few of them in the name of our worldly orthodoxy. ~ A.W. Tozer

➤ And the LORD answered me, and said, write the vision, and make [it] plain upon tables, that he may run that readeth it. ~ Habakkuk 2:2 KJV

➤ People buy into the leader before they buy into the vision. ~ John C. Maxwell

➤ Where there is no vision, there is no hope. ~ George Washington Carver

➢ It is not expedient for me doubtless to glory. I will come to visions and revelations of the Lord. ~2 Corinthians 12:1 KJV

➢ The most pathetic person in the world is someone who has sight, but has no vision. ~ Helen Keller

➢ I'm thankful that I came of age politically in the era of Ronald Reagan, in high school and college. He is my inspiration. His vision of America and of the exceptional-ism of our country. I think about him every day. I think about what that Great Communicator has left our country and the rest of the world. ~ Sarah Palin

➢ And it shall come to pass afterward, [that] I will pour out my spirit upon all flesh; and your sons and your daughters shall prophesy, your old men shall dream dreams, your young men shall see visions. ~ Joel 2:28 KJV

➢ Solemnized by the knowledge of the deep need and inspired by the vision of all things made new by the mighty Christ, resolve to give yourselves to encouraging a spiritual awakening. ~ John R. Mott

➢ What a curious workmanship is that of the eye, which is in the body, as the sun in the world; set in the head as in a watch-tower, having the softest nerves for receiving the greater multitude of spirits necessary for the act of vision! ~ Stephan Charnock

➢ And a vision appeared to Paul in the night; There stood a man of Macedonia, and prayed him, saying, Come over into Macedonia, and help us. ~ Acts 16:9 KJV

➤ When one door closes, another opens, but we so often look upon the closed door that we do not see the one that has opened for us. ~ Alexander Graham Bell

➤ You are not here merely to make a living. You are here in order to enable the world to live more amply, with greater vision, with a finer spirit of hope and achievement. You are here to enrich the world, and you impoverish yourself if you forget the errand. ~ Woodrow Wilson

➤ Vision gets the dreams started. Dreaming employs your God-given imagination to reinforce the vision. Both are part of something I believe is absolutely necessary to building the life of a champion, a winner, a person of high character who is consistently at the top of whatever game he or she is in. ~ Emmitt Smith

➢ The only way the corporate Body of Christ will fulfill the mission Christ has given it is for individual Christians to have a vision for fulfilling that mission personally. ~ David Jeremiah

➢ When a plan or strategy fails, people are tempted to assume it was the wrong vision. Plans and strategies can always be changed and improved. But vision doesn't change. Visions are simply refined with time. ~ Andy Stanley

➢ Where [there is] no vision, the people perish: but he that keepeth the law, happy [is] he. ~ Proverbs 29:18 KJV

Let's find your perfect combination. These are two visions you can work on at the same time because they complement each other. See page 10.

## LIST 3 THINGS YOU WANT TO DO

Example: Meet the President of the United States

1) _____

2) _____

3) _____

## LIST 3 THINGS YOU WANT TO BECOME

Example: Become the Mayor of my City

1) _____

2) _____

3) _____

# PICK ONE FROM EACH LIST & LIST BELOW:

1) _____

2) _____

Example:

   1) <u>Meet the President of the United States</u>
   2) <u>Become the Mayor of my City</u>

*This is your perfect combination.*

## NOW WRITE YOUR VISION FOR EACH:

My vision for #1 is:

_____

_____

_____

_____

_____

My vision for #2 is:

_____

_____

_____

_____

_____

What will you have to do to make this happen?

Vision #1: *(Example: Write a letter to the White House)*

_____

_____

_____

_____

_____

_____

_____

_____

_____

_____

Vision #2: *(Example: Study politics and government)*

_____

_____

_____

_____

_____

_____

_____

_____

_____

Now it's all up to you to do it!
Make the visions collide for a *perfect combination.*

# Chapter 2
# Creating a Vision Board

There are many ways vision is inspired; however, I would like to suggest that every visionary needs a vision board. You can have daily steps toward accomplishing your vision or weekly steps you take during the school year. Now that you have an idea of what a vision is and how it is developed, we need to create and make a vision board. A vision board is a visual map or view of what you are trying to create. It helps to see where you want to go and what you want to do. It also helps to take another look at your vision from the outside looking in.

A vision board is exactly what it sounds like; it is a board that you put together to see yourself in the future. It kind of helps you out if you are a visual learner. It also helps those who are not visual learners as I believe that if you can see your vision, it helps you to remain encouraged to pursue your dreams. First, here is an example of my vision board and how I see what my future will look like in the next ten years or so:

These are all things that I want to happen in my life ahead; these are my visions. As you can see, I want to dance for fun and make music because it's what I live for. I want to be a businesswoman with my own medical center, have a great education, and a healthy family. Now clearly, everything that I want to happen is definitely not going to happen exactly the way I dream of it happening. But then again, this is just my guide to follow. While you create your vision board, remember that there will be times that things won't happen the way you visualized it, but that doesn't mean it won't happen at all.

Another realistic example is a demonstration of a girl named Kelly Mantu. Her vision board shares how she dreams of the future ahead. She wants to do just a few things, but you will later see how she had to narrow it down. Kelly has 3 goals for her adult life after her last year of high school. She wants to get her high school diploma *(goal 1)*, *she* wants to go to college *(goal 2)*, and she wants to be famous soccer player *(goal 3)*.

What do you see here? All of them are labeled according to what she wants to accomplish first. This is the exact thing you want to do because it helps with the order you want your life to go in. It's the perfect example of one of the decisions you need to make. If you have no order, you have no plan. If you have no plan, what's on your vision board will never happen. Ask yourself these questions and make sure that you are on the right track.

I remembered the summer I made a tough decision about whether to continue with dance (which I had been doing for about seven to eight years) or choose to play tennis (which I had been playing for only one summer but was very skillful). I chose dance, but when I look back over that summer, I could've participated in both with a little planning. I was just so stumped at the time and put under so much pressure, that I made a quick decision without having a vision board to look at. If I had a little more order to my life, I would've been able to see what I really wanted to accomplish by the end of the summer.

Anyway, here's Kelly's vision board:

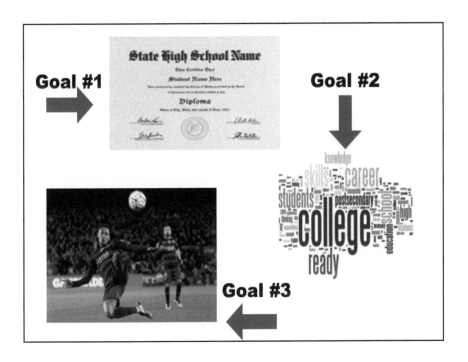

Now, this is Kelly's example of her vision board and how she wants her life to turn out. Kelly wants to be a strong young lady who has a great existence. She wants people to have the same strength when they see her. I admire Kelly because Kelly only wants to be the best she can be.

I want you to make the commitment to be yourself, not anyone else. We have too many young people trying to be like people they see on T.V. Everybody wants to be on top and be filthy rich. Don't get me wrong. I don't think anything is wrong with this. It's just that most of the time people do it the wrong way or for a selfish reason. Whatever we do, we should do it unto God, giving Him all the praise and thanksgiving for the vision He gave.

Now, back to Kelly. Kelly wants to get her high school diploma, go to college, and become a professional soccer player. It looks like Kelly has a lot on her plate, but don't worry because she has order to her vision. We'll talk about this more in the next chapter. It will show you how to "bring down" your choices to decide what to do and how to make it happen.

Now that you have seen an example from not only my perspective but from Kelly's viewpoint, I want you to make your own vision board. Are you ready? I hope you answered, yes! Before you get there, I want to give you my five vision rules:

1. Make sure your goals inspire you. If you're inspired, other people will be inspired by you.

2. Set S.M.A.R.T. goals. This is something I learned really early in school. The acronym S.M.A.R.T. stands for goals that are: Specific, Measurable, Attainable, Relevant, and Time-Bound.

3. Always put your goals in writing. I know you will have pictures on your vision board, but you should also write them down in your notebook or journal.

4. Once you know what you want to do, make a plan to do it.

5. No matter what, don't quit!

Here are two other pointers before you start making your vision board:

1. Invite a few friends to make their vision board with you. You got it, have a vision party!

2. Use Google and Pinterest to see more examples of vision boards.

Alright, I think we're ready. Let's get started on making our vision boards.

# Create your VISION BOARD

Follow these Steps:

1. Make a list of everything you want to do or become.

2. Find pictures (use lots of magazines) that represent what you have on the list you created. For example: If you want to be a doctor, find pictures of doctors.

3. You will need cardstock or poster paper. The average size is 20x30, but your paper can be as small or large as you like. Be sure to have glue and markers.

4. Cut the images from the magazines and glue them on your vision board.

5. Don't forget to put them in order like Kelly did. What do you want to do first, second, and third?

6. It's really cool if you paste a picture of yourself in the middle of your vision board. This reminds you that your vision board is a reflection of what you see.

**More on the next page**

7. Now, hang the vision board up in a place where you can see it often. Stay true to yourself and work toward what you see.

# Chapter 3
## Bring it Down

So far, we have talked about what a vision is and what it means. You now know what a vision board is and how to use it when it comes to making big decisions. Now that we've finished deciding what you plan to do in the future, it's time to do the process of elimination. What do I mean by this? I mean that you need to cut things that might seem important but really doesn't agree with who you want to be in the future or what you want to do.

If your vision board looks anything like mine, you probably have pictures of your future everywhere. Look really close to figure out the things that are best for what you feel like you really want to do. When you scan your vision board to decide, make sure this is actually what you want to do and that it's not just for fortune or fame. Whatever you decide to do in the future, make sure that you can proudly say, "I did this because I knew the vision for my life and wanted to fulfill my purpose."

Listen clearly, in order to bring down your top choices; you have to understand that you can't major in five, six, seven, or eight things. It kind of goes back to what my mother told me. You have to focus on what you are supposed to be doing now. You might have a few minors, but you should narrow your major goals down.

Man, doesn't this feel good to have some focus and direction even at our age. You can stay in this place if you constantly ask yourself these questions, what do I love to do? What am I always attracted to? What can I understand right off the bat; and what can I easily memorize? How many times a day do I think about this? What excites me and prevents me from becoming bored? If you look for the answers to these questions, you will find what you really want to do.

If you're like me, you can get so excited that you just want to take a walk into the future and live the life you see. Bring it down! There are lots of choices to make and things to experience before we both get there. One thing to always take on this journey is honesty. There it is again! Be honest with yourself. Denying that you want to do something because you're scared that you will fail or fearful of what people will say, will always hold you back. Don't step into your future hurt and mad, but fix it now if this is where you are. Just be honest with yourself.

Back to my realistic example about Kelly in Chapter 2. Let's say that Kelly wanted to originally do five things but had to choose because she can only do two. Initially, Kelly wanted to play soccer, volleyball, baseball, tennis, and be on the dance team. In fact, she was almost a perfectionist at all of them but had to choose one. She had to bring it down showing us that life does come with tough choices.

This is where being honest really matters. We all know that Kelly chose soccer, but what if she didn't make this her choice. What if she chose tennis just because she wanted to meet Serena Williams? I think she would've discovered that she didn't have as much passion as she does for soccer. She would've failed at being a great soccer player because she didn't chose to do what she loved. After you make your decision from all the options you have, ask yourself, "what made me believe that this is for me? Will I feel bad about my choice in the future?"

See, Kelly made the right choice because she knew how to bring it down. She chose to do what made the most sense for where she wanted to be in the future. She made the connection between how what she does now will impact her future. When you are done reading this book, continue to ask the questions I gave you. It will help bring down the important things within your vision.

# Chapter 4
# What is Collision?

In this case, a collision is when a variety of things collide and make up some kind of reaction. The reason I explain it the way I do is because this is a simple word that if used elsewhere, it could mean something bad. Almost like when you hear that cars collided in an accident; the outcome is bad. You see, for the most part, collision is viewed as being not so good. However, in this case, it will have a positive outcome.

The things that you want to collide are the things that will benefit and have good outcomes on the goals you have. What happens, in this case, is everything you see, collides with one another; this is *vision collision*. While it might seem chaotic, it's really good because everything is going to work toward your vision and what you have on your vision board.

When vision and collision are combined, it helps to see what's coming in your future. Vision = what you see; Collision = what comes together. The meaning of both words makes you really think about what you want to happen when the connection of the two take place. You want to be able to see where you are starting, what's in between, and what's coming.

If you really take time to think about your moment of vision collision, it will help you to know if you are missing anything in your plan. If you see what you want and how it all comes together, but still missing something, the collision will never take place. It's almost like getting in the car to go to the store with my mom, and we don't have gas. My dad has to make sure gas is in the car so that we can make it to the store. Without gas, we will never get there. You see, my mom can envision us being at the store, but we won't experience vision collision if we are missing gas.

Vision collision helps to know what your beginning and ending looks like. For example, I want to major in business and music even though they seem to be totally opposite of each other. But when I practice the method of bring it down, they both actually help my vision to collide in the future because I want to help music artist in the industry. There's a connection between the two. This is what you want to find because the connection sets you up for the collision.

If I look at my vision board and choose to focus on business and music, it will help me to become the boss. I like that! I will not only know what it takes to run a business like this but will also know all the rules that singers and songwriters must go by. In this case, this is my perfect combination because when the two of them collide together, my vision comes to past. Oh, one last thing about your connection. Make sure you find the strongest connection and don't settle for the simplest connection. Why? Because you will regret it knowing that you could have done better.

So to sum it up, you want to find a good way for your ideas to collide and make magic. Don't make this more difficult than it should be. Stop to think about one good idea you have. Pause, think about the other good idea you have. Now, think about the day they will both collide together to make your vision come to past. Make sure you know where you want to go and what you want to do. If you stay focused on the plan to accomplish both, your visions are sure to have a collision.

# Chapter 5
# Making the Vision work

YAY! The final step, PUTTING IT ALL TOGETHER. If we review our journey so far, we would know that in order to experience vision collision, you have to: (1) have a vision, (2) understand your vision, (3) make it collide with another idea, and (4) follow your dreams.

Here are the last two examples from Kelly and myself. We already know Kelly's plan and what she wants to do, but now we need to ask what she did to get to vision collision. Kelly made her vision board but now had to decide when to put her vision into action. Just in case you didn't know, timing is everything.

As you know, Kelly wanted to do a lot but had to narrow it down to one or two things. She did this by imagining what would fit into her vision to have the easiest collision. She chose soccer and college. This made it easy for her to attend college and play soccer at the same time. Playing soccer while in college could prepare her to play professionally after college. What a vision collision!

Honestly, from my point of view, I think Kelly made the right choice. Why? Because her decision came from her heart. It was based on what she loves to do, and where she sees herself in the future. She decided to do what she loved, and it was probably much easier for her to love her surroundings and the people in it. I'm sure that making the right choice required not listening to what and where people wanted her life to go. She likely got advice from a few smart people, as you should do, but she didn't allow their advice to totally influence her vision.

As I said before, life comes with very tough choices. Believe me because I know and I've made some myself even being so young. I can only imagine the choices that wait for you and me in the future. Whatever the future holds, it's up to you to make the right choices. You can only do this with the help of God. This is not to say that both you and I won't make wrong decisions in our future. However, if we put God first, He will never watch the situation beat us up. God will always provide help to make the right moves, to get you to where he wants you to be. Don't worry, He's patient with us and knows that there's still some work you have to do to grow.

There's a story in the Bible that tells the story of the Parables of the Talents (Matthew 25-14-30). Here's what the story is about. There once was a master and his servants. The servants, you know, cleaned the house and whatnot. Well, the master wanted to go on a long vacation so he asked his servants to make sure that they could care for the house and keep it in good shape while he was gone.

Keep thinking about how we, the people, are the servants, and God is the master. I also want to throw in an example one of my aunts told me about when telling this story. She said that it's like a checker game between God and the devil. We are the pieces, and they are the players. Another way I like to think of this is like a basketball game. We are the ball, and the person with the ball has control over the focus of the game.

You get it? Great! Let's get back to the story. The master decided to give each of the servants some kind of talent, and to some He gave more than others. He gave the first man five talents, which probably could've earned him five million dollars. Oh, keep in mind that the Master gave the servants these talents based on what He thought each servant could handle.

With the second man, he gave him two talents because this is what the master thought that he would be able to handle. The third man was given one talent, to see what he could do. Right away, almost all of the servants did something with the talents they were given. The man with the five talents used his talents and got five more. He must've known the art of making vision collision happen. The man with the two talents did the same. He went out, used his talents and got two more.

There was something odd about the third man that threw me off. He absolutely didn't use his talent at all. He decided to hide it under some dirt because he lacked vision for his future. This surprised me because obviously, the master gave him the talent because he believed in him. Can you believe this servant? He did not try to use his talent at all. He just hid his talent under dirt!

After a nice long and relaxing vacation, the master came back hoping to be impressed with the servants. He was very pleased to know that the first servant with the five talents used what he gave him. The master trusted him to do something, and he did just that. The master told the servant, "Great job, you good and faithful servant."

After this, the master took a look at the second servant. He was pleased that the second one used both of his talents and received two more. The master once again said," Great job, you good and faithful servant." Can you imagine how proud he was with the two who worked their vision? On the other hand, he was extremely disappointed that the third servant did not even consider doing anything with his talents. He had no vision and buried all of his potential under dirt. The servant blamed it on fear, but the master told him that he was 100% lazy. You know what happened? The master took away his one talent and gave it to the first man making him have eleven talents. I'm disappointed in the third servant as well. I wish he had read this book before he went to bury his talent. He would've known that even if you don't have a lot on your vision board, you can still create a vision collision if you pursue even the smallest thing that you see in your future.

I told you this story hoping that you really understand that God gives you gifts because He knows that you can handle the vision He has for your life. God never gives you anything with the expectation that you will fail. He will always make sure it's easy enough for you to carry out. Now I didn't say it would be easy, but if you carry your vision, it's easier than trying to carry the vision that belongs to someone else. God is looking and smiling from heaven because he knows that you can fulfill this vision. Otherwise, He would have never allowed the thought to enter your mind. Trust me; you can do this!

God gave me, remember a 12-year-old, a vision to throw a Harvest party at church for all of the kids. I knew it was going to be overwhelming and stressful, but somehow, I did it. I listened to what God was saying and listened to how He said to do it. In the end, everything worked out perfectly. You see, God just wants to know if you will use your gift to fulfill His vision.

Most people think that all young people these days do is play video games, watch TV, and post on social media. I happen to believe that there are young people who are not so entertained by things that don't help us to be better in the future. I think both you and I are a part of the group of young people that have made up in our minds to use the gifts God has given us.

I'm really excited about God giving us more to fulfill the big vision He has. I want to be like the servant with the ten talents or even the one with two talents. Both of them used what they had and received more to have a bigger impact and to become better people.

Guess what? A lot of young people our age don't know what their vision is. Don't look down or tease them. After you know your vision, help them discover their vision. In fact, look for the gifts in others, so that you can help make their vision clear to them. Make them feel happy and proud to know that all young people aren't so much into technology that we forget to care for people. Come on, help me let them know that there is a little bit of the old time ways in us! Use your talents for good, not for evil. Most importantly, use your talents unto GOD!

Just in case you don't read the story I told you about in the bible, I wanted to put it in this book to make it easier for you to read. Check this out:

Matthew 25: 14-30 (MSG)

It's also like a man going off on an extended trip. He called his servants together and delegated responsibilities. To one he gave five thousand dollars, to another two thousand, to a third one thousand, depending on their abilities. Then he left. Right off, the first servant went to work and doubled his master's investment. The second did the same. But the man with the single thousand dug a hole and carefully buried his master's money. After a long absence, the master of those three servants came back and settled up with them. The one given five thousand dollars showed him how he had doubled his investment. His master commended him: 'Good work! You did your job well. From now on, be my partner.' The servant with the two thousand showed how he also had doubled his master's investment. His master commended him: 'Good work! You did your job well. From now on be my partner.' The servant given one thousand said, 'Master, I know you have high standards and hate careless ways, that you demand the best and make no allowances for error. I was afraid I might disappoint you, so I found a good hiding place and secured your money. Here it is, safe and sound down to the last cent.'

The master was furious. 'That's a terrible way to live! It's criminal to live cautiously like that! If you knew I was after the best, why did you do less than the least? The least you could have done would have been to invest the sum with the bankers, where at least I would have gotten a little interest. Take the thousand and give it to the one who risked the most. And get rid of this "play-it-safe" who won't go out on a limb. Throw him out into utter darkness.'

# Conclusion

OMG! Can you believe that we have come to the end of our vision collision journey? At least the part where we do this together; now it's all on you. You have to take what you've learned and apply it to your life. Remember, never allow age or circumstance to hold you back. I salute my grandma, Marie, who went back to school as a single parent of five small children, graduated at the top of the class with a 3.95 GPA, and successfully retired in that very field. I also salute both of my grandfathers that went back to school and earned bachelor's degrees later in life. You can do it. Remember, I'm twelve years old and wrote this book because of the vision that God gave me.

I just believe that no matter how old or young a person is, they can accomplish anything that they set their mind to. If you think it, you will begin to see yourself being just that in the future. Once you see it and imagine it, you know what happens from there. You now have a vision that you have to fulfill.

Be sure to write your vision on paper so that you don't forget what you see. I challenge you to show the vision board you created to some of your friends. I guarantee that they will want one too. You should get everyone together and have a vision board party. Why do this? Because not only were you called to fulfill your vision, but you are supposed to help someone along the way.

It's a good time during the vision party for you and your friends to help each other bring it down. Remember, you can't do everything you see at one time. You have to put your goals in order and work on the visions you're supposed to work on now so that the visions of the future will collide in time. Vision collision is what you're after. You may identify several things you want to do but just make sure that what you do now, will make you happy and fulfilled later.

I really pray that you enjoyed this book. I'm still in awe that I am a young published author. I still see so much, and I strongly believe that this is just the beginning of God's vision for me to be an author that writes empowering books to help others. I know that what I'm writing now will collide with books I write in the future.

I'm super grateful that you were with me from the beginning of this journey. I hope we are still connected when everything collides together. In fact, I want to witness the vision collision of your dreams. The only way you will get there is if you use your talents like you were born to do! Be true to yourself and rock your vision like a rock star because when you have vision, that's exactly what you are.

## LET'S STAY CONNECTED
If you need help making your vision board or would like me to host a vision board party, email me: **visioncollision12@gmail.com**

# VISION COLLISION

**THINK • WRITE • BELIEVE • ACHIEVE**